create your own...
BOUTIQUE

Marta Dansa
text by Gina Samba

First American Edition 2016
Kane Miller, A Division of EDC Publishing

Copyright © Edicions Somnins 2010 S.L.
Illustrations copyright © Marta Dansa
Text copyright © Gina Samba

First published by Edicions Somnins 2010

somnins

For information contact:
Kane Miller, A Division of EDC Publishing
PO Box 470663
Tulsa, OK 74147-0663
www.kanemiller.com
www.edcpub.com
www.usbornebooksandmore.com

Library of Congress Control Number: 2015954217

Manufactured by Regent Publishing Services, Hong Kong
Printed March 2016 in ShenZhen, Guangdong, China

1 2 3 4 5 6 7 8 9 10

ISBN: 978-1-61067-440-9

Hi! I'm
Martina.*

And I'm*
Pablo.

create your own ...
BOUTIQUE

With this book, you'll plan and design your very own fashion boutique!

You get to pick a name, decide on the decor, choose your fixtures and figure out what you'll carry in your store.

When you're done, prepare your catalog, unlock the door and get ready for your customers!

*Martina and Pablo are here to help.

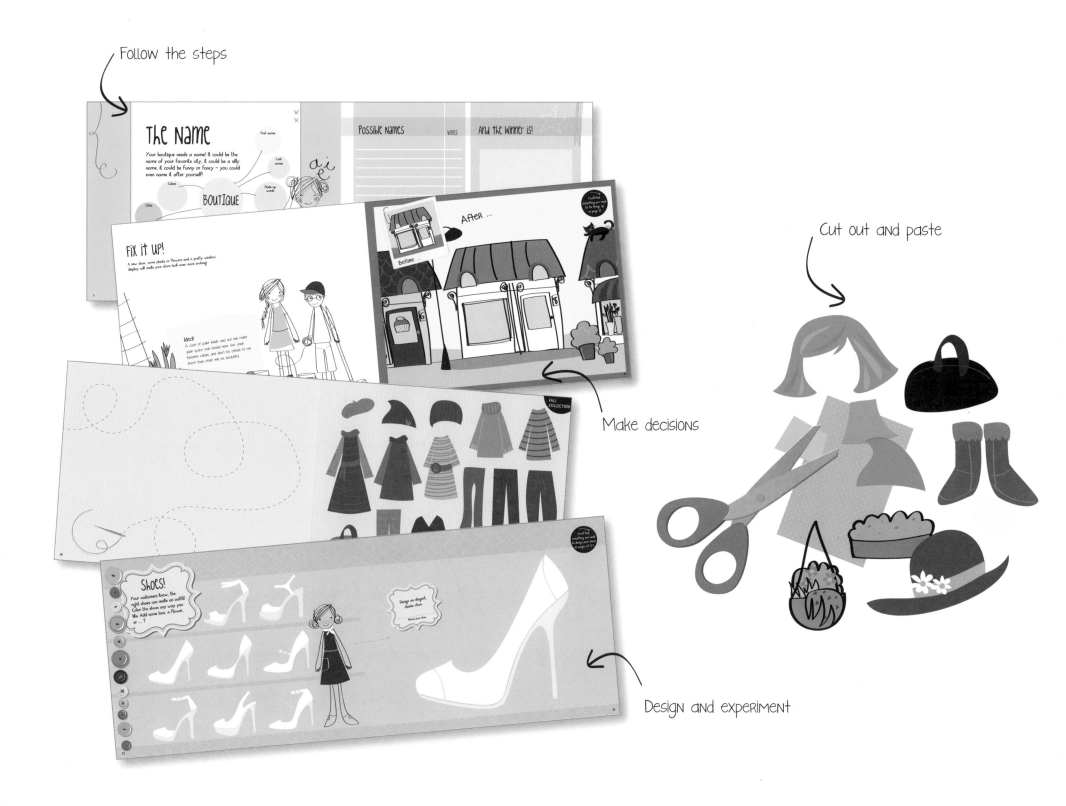

Follow the steps

THE NAME

Your boutique needs a name! It could be the name of your favorite city, it could be a silly name, it could be funny or fancy — you could even name it after yourself!

First names

Last names

Colors

Made-up words

Cities

BOUTIQUE

Possible names	VOTES	And the winner is!

Cut out and paste

FIX IT UP!

A new door, some plants or flowers and a pretty window display will make your store look even more inviting!

Before

After ...

Idea!
A coat of paint inside and out will make your space look brand new. Use your favorite colors and don't be afraid to mix them! Your store will be beautiful.

Make decisions

FALL COLLECTION

SHOES!

Your customers know, the right shoes can make an outfit! Color the shoes any way you like. Add some lace, a flower, or ...?

Design an elegant, classic shoe.

Name your shoe

Design and experiment

3

THE NAME

Your boutique needs a name! It could be the name of your favorite city, it could be a silly name, it could be funny or fancy — you could even name it after yourself!

First names
Jules

Last names
D'Andrea

Colors
Purple
Blue
aqua

BOUTIQUE

Made-up words
Monyagon
lefefal
loblaboothlah

Cities
Boston
NYC
Providence

Flowers
Rose
Dasiy
Lailac

The White Orchid Boutique

Pretty words
Beautiful
Mademie
Coragous

Paris BOUTIQUE

COCOLOO

Possible Names

	VOTES
NYC of beautiful Boutic	30
The Aqua State Boutic	5
Coragous Rose Boutic	10
Mademé Lailac Boutic	32
Boston Lailac Boutic	31
Providence of the D'Andreas	9
Boston lefefal Nyc	0
Jules is Beautiful	1
Jules mademé	0
aqua dandred	2

Ask your friends and family to vote for the name they like the best.

And the winner is!

The Logo

Designing a logo for your store is an important step. Using your logo on your catalog, signs and elsewhere helps identify your business and show everyone what it's all about.

Pick a background, add the name of your store and then choose an image (or two)!

You'll find everything you need on page 31.

There are so many possibilities!

Images to add

Write the name of your boutique.

6

Lettering Style

The name of your boutique is the most important part of your logo. Try out different lettering styles — does plain, fancy, decorated or simple make it look best?

Practice different styles and designs on a piece of paper, then paste your finished logo below.

Location! Location! Location!

Choosing the right location for a store isn't easy, but don't worry! The perfect spot could be just around the corner ...

Fix it up!

A new door, some plants or flowers and a pretty window display will make your store look even more inviting!

Idea!

A coat of paint inside and out will make your space look brand new. Use your favorite colors and don't be afraid to mix them! Your store will be beautiful.

After ...

Before ...

You'll find everything you need to fix things up on page 33.

clothes and accessories

It's your store — you decide which clothes and accessories you'll carry each season, and which you'll feature in your catalog and window displays.

collections

Designers offer new clothing collections each season. Which pieces will you choose for spring, summer, fall and winter? It's hard to decide ...

Which is your favorite season? Showcase the clothes in your catalog.

You'll find everything you need for spring and summer on pages 35-37.

A scarf can be the perfect accessory!

Spring collection

14

Sunglasses are a must!

SUMMER COLLECTION

You'll find everything you need for fall and winter on pages 39-41.

Oranges and browns are the perfect colors for fall.

Fall collection

Combine bold reds with cool grays for something new.

Winter collection

Your own designs

You'll find what you need on pages 43-46.

Sometimes you want something totally different (and so do your customers)!
Use the paper "fabrics" on pages 43-46 as you design and name your favorite dresses.

Pattern Notebook

Cocktail dresses
Short, colorful party dresses

Evening dresses
Long and dramatic, these make a statement.

Choose your fabric, sketch the design and cut it out. You can create whatever you like: skirts, tops, belts, jackets ... whatever you can imagine!

Name your designs.

Ask your friends and family to choose, and record their favorites from 1 to 10.

Name your designs.

Name your designs.

Shoes!

Your customers know, the right shoes can make an outfit! Color the shoes any way you like. Add some lace, a flower, or ... ?

You'll find everything you need to design your shoes on pages 47-51.

Design an elegant, classic shoe.

....
Name your shoe.

Design a cool summer sandal.

Name your shoe.

Design a sky-high, party shoe.

Name your shoe.

1 You can't do it all

A boutique as special as yours will require an excellent staff of salespeople, supervisors, stylists and models. Let's get started!

Your staff

Attach photos or draw pictures of the people who'll make up your staff. They could be friends, relatives, or even people you haven't met yet! What a great team!

Owner

Manager

Seamstress

Stylist

Salesperson

Salesperson

Salesperson

The Stylist

Your stylist will help customers shopping for specific occasions or events. It's fun, and it's harder than you think! Dress the model on the left in the worst outfit you can come up with. Dress the model on the right in the best outfit. Are they closer than you thought?

You'll find everything you need on page 53.

Oh, no!

Beautiful! It's perfect!

The Seamstress

Your seamstress will tailor customers' purchases for a perfect fit. Hemming, taking in, letting out, changing buttons — she can alter it all!

⚠️ A grown-up should be present when you try this for the first time.

Everyone needs to know how to sew on a button! Study the drawings and follow the steps. Remember to be careful with the needle.

1   2   3   4   5

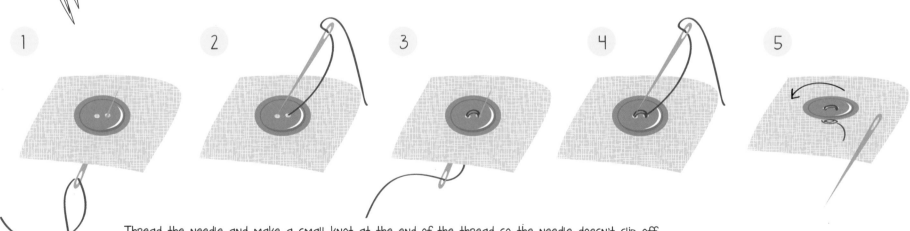

Thread the needle and make a small knot at the end of the thread so the needle doesn't slip off.

Place the button where you'd like it, then hold it as you sew up through the fabric and a button hole.

Go down through the other button hole, through the fabric.

Repeat these steps until the button is tight to the fabric.

Make a small knot in the thread on the underside of the cloth. Snip the excess thread and voila! You've sewn on a button.

Patterns, papers and designs

Use the small pictures for your logo.

Save the larger ones for your catalog.

32

A new roof can make a big difference.

Pretty awnings look nice and help protect your stock from bright sunlight.

What about a colored door?

33

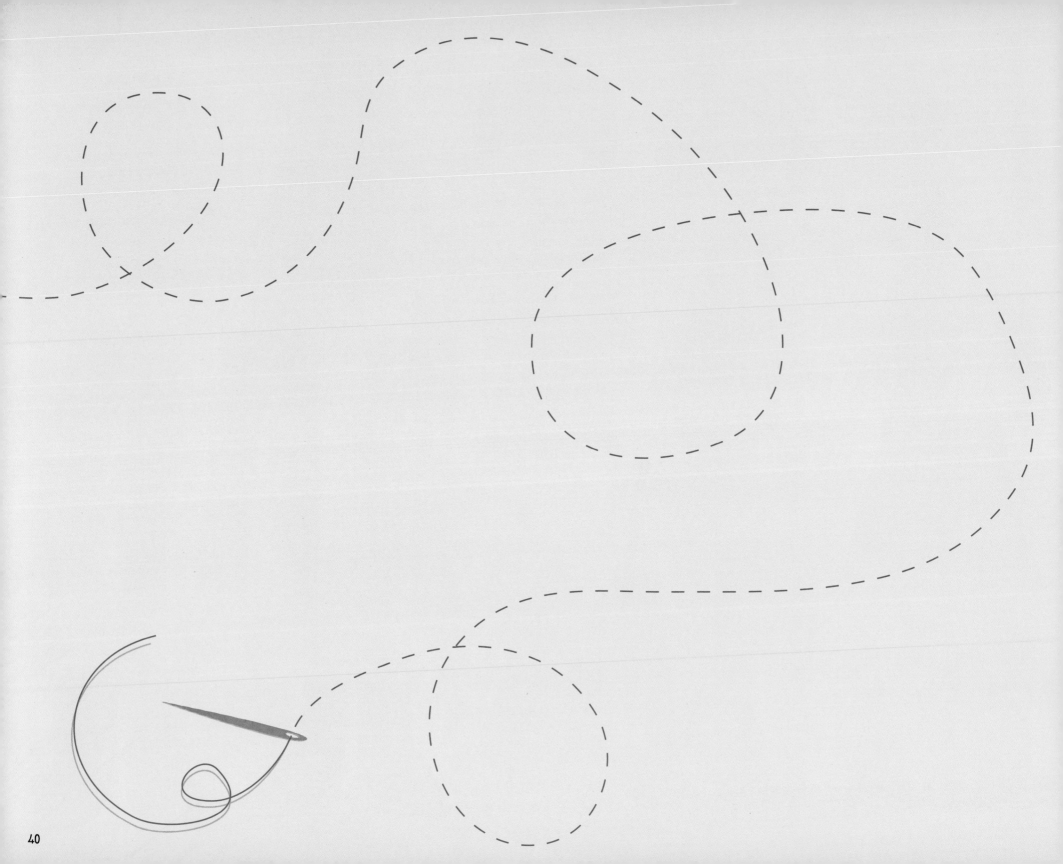

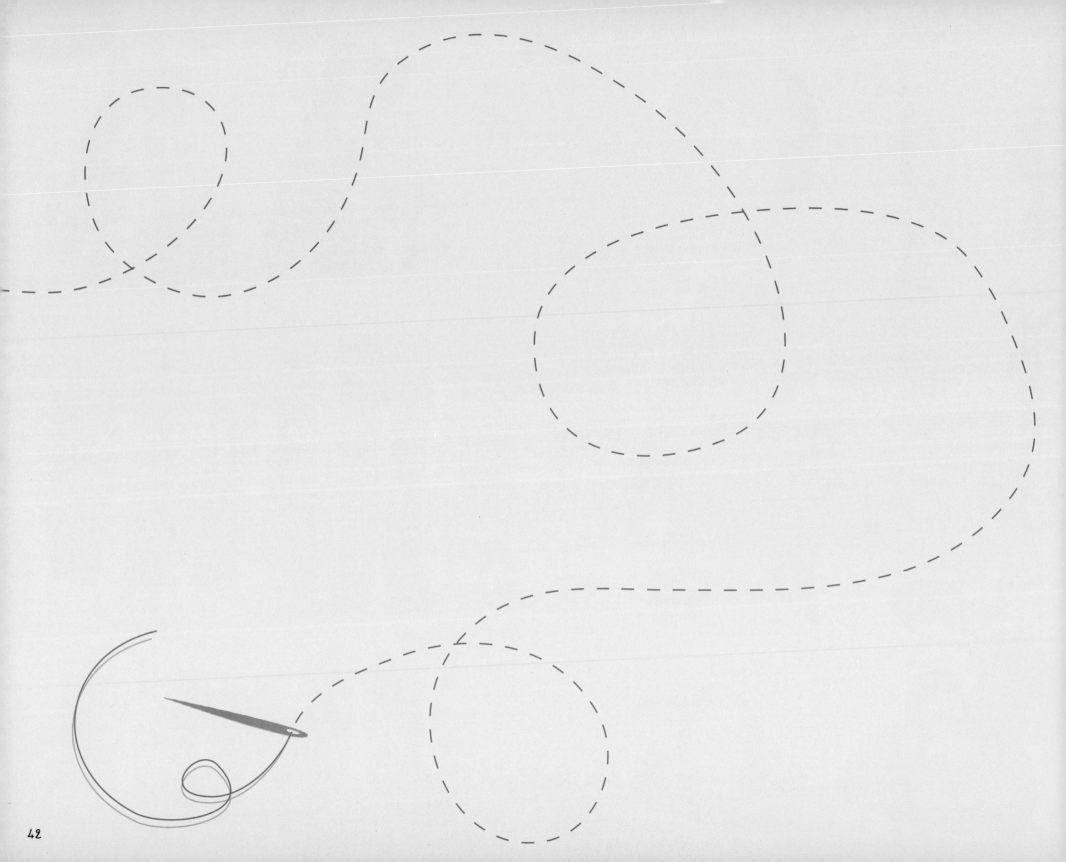

You can cut out this dress form to use as a template.

44

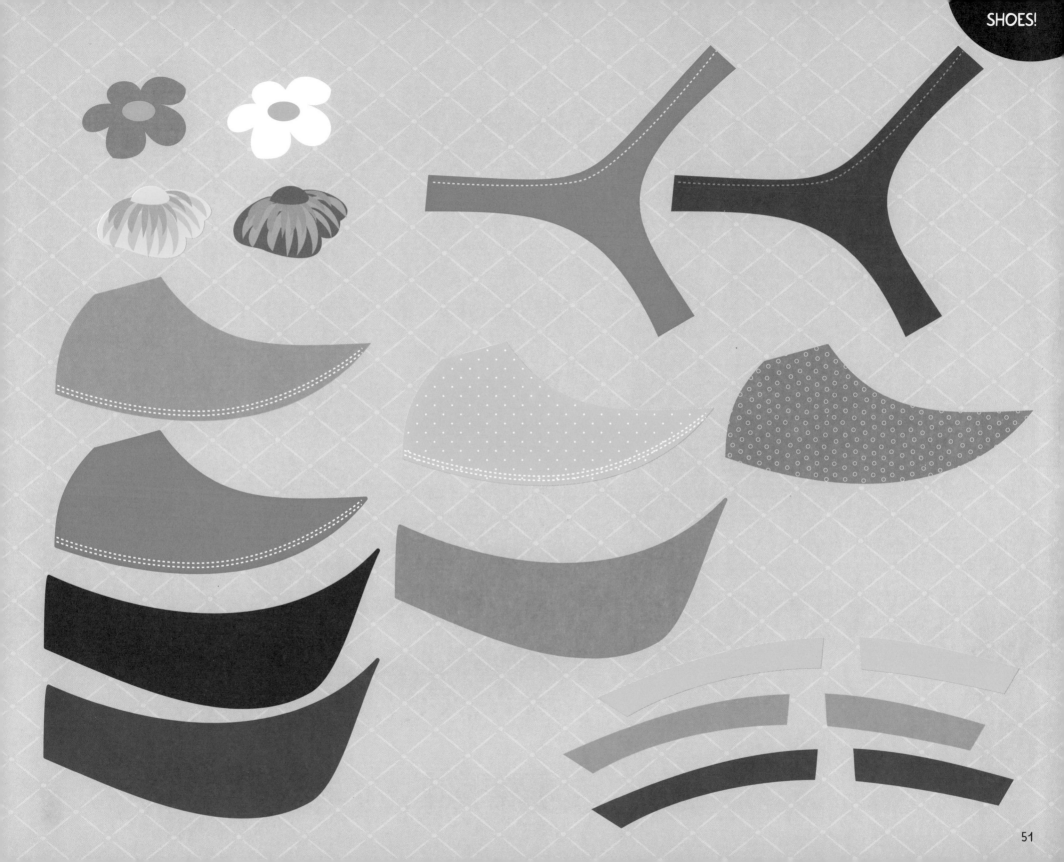

CATALOG

DESIGN YOUR CATALOG

You have the perfect space and the perfect name. You've hired your staff and stocked your boutique with the best clothing and accessories. Now it's time to share your beautiful creations in your store catalog!

your boutique CATALOG

Choose and attach ...

You'll find everything you need to create your catalog on the following pages.

You can offer other pieces from the collections as specials.

A picture of your store

Write the address and telephone number of your boutique. Draw a map too, so customers can find you.

The outfit you like best for the stylist section

Styling Services

Special offers

We look forward to seeing you!

You'll find us at:

Telephone:

Paris
BOUTIQUE

Your logo

CATALOG

Favorite pieces from the collections

New collection

custom work

Accessories

Don't forget accessories!

The best of the best

An original design

56

Storefronts and accessories

modern

urban

classic

playful

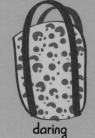
daring

alternative

eco-fashion

trendy

unique

youthful

elegant

spacious

functional

serious

professional

sporty

comfortable

modern

career

chic

Special occasions

Customizable wedding dresses and evening gowns

Style services

We show you how to put together an outfit.